W9-BLB-977

Little Wolf's

Diary of

Daring Deeds

Ian Whybrow
Illustrated by Tony Ross

Carolrhoda Books, Inc., Minneapolis

HAMNEEZIA

SPOOKE

MT. FARVIEW

WH

GRIM MOUNTAINS

MT. SKYWARD

MT. TESTER

BROKEN
TOOTH
CAVES

BEASTSHIR

DARK HILLS

W

E

S

WINDY RIDGE

FRETININ
FOREST

CUNNING COLLEGE

ADVENTURE
ACADEMY

LAKE
LEMMING

RIVER RIGGL

Sc

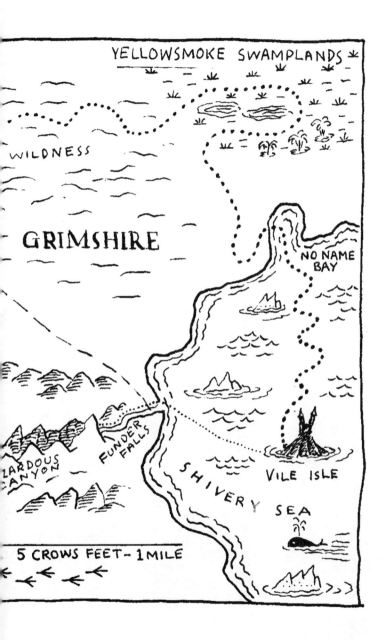

This American edition published in 2000 by Carolrhoda Books, Inc.

Text copyright © by Ian Whybrow 1996
Illustrations copyright © by Tony Ross 1996

Published by arrangement with HarperCollins Publishers Ltd, London,
England. Originally published in English by HarperCollins Publishers Ltd
under the title LITTLE WOLF'S DIARY OF DARING DEEDS.

The Author and Illustrator assert the moral right
to be identified as the Author and Illustrator of the work.

Carolrhoda Books, Inc.
A division of Lerner Publishing Group
241 First Avenue North
Minneapolis, MN 55401 U.S.A.

Website address: www.lernerbooks.com

Library of Congress Cataloging-in-Publication Data
Whybrow, Ian.
Little Wolf's diary of daring deeds / Ian Whybrow ; illustrated
by Tony Ross.
p. cm.
Summary: In letters home to Mom and Dad, Little Wolf describes his
journey to rescue his little brother, Smellybreff, from a crafty cubnapper,
Mister Twister the Fox.
ISBN 1-57505-411-6 (lib. bdg. : alk. paper)
[1. Wolves—Fiction. 2. Brothers—Fiction. 3. Foxes—Fiction. 4. Rescues—
Fiction. 5. Letters—Fiction.] I. Ross, Tony, ill. II. Title.

PZ7.W6225 Lk 2000
[Fic]—dc21   99-053204
Manufactured in the United States of America

2 3 4 5 6 7—QB—06 05 04 03 02 01

ADVENTURE ACADEMY

~~CUNNING COLLEGE FOR BRUTE BEASTS,~~

FOR DARING DEEDERS
FRETTNIN FOREST, BEASTSHIRE
~~BIGBAD WOLF, ESQ~~

HEADS: LITTLE WOLF AND YELLER WOLF, ESQS

Better, huh?

Dear Mom and Dad,

Please please PLEEEEEZ come and move in here. You said you would! My cuz Yeller is coming soonly, then we will get some pupils and start up Adventure Academy at last!!

I cannot wait. I have found bags and bags of gold that Uncle Bigbad hid. That means I am RICH!! So we are going to have the best, most fun school ever. Also, we are going to buy the best adventures in the world and put them in our playground. Then we can do daring deeds all the time. Arrrooo!

5

I want you to come so you can be proud of me. Dad can retire from his work at Fang and Mauler and put his paws up. I have made the cellar all nice and smelly for you just like the lair.

Tell Smellybreff that yes, he can be a teacher because he is my baby bro, but remember, me and Yeller are pack leaders, so no moaning.

Yours hurryuply,

Little

P.S. I am sending you some more gold so you can come by helicopter.

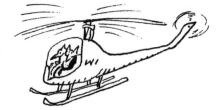

ADVENTURE ACADEMY

FRETTNIN FOREST, BEASTSHIRE
HEADS: LITTLE WOLF AND YELLER WOLF, ESQS

Dear Mom and Dad,

Nifty notepaper, huh?

Big winds in the night. Tell the helicopter pilot I am wurrid about him not seeing which part of the forest to come down in. So I have written HELLO, HELLY, LAND ON YOUR BELLY on a big sign for him.

Still no Yeller. Boo, shame. Where is he? I wish he would hurry up, because his ideas are just the best. Also, I need him to help me with slogans for our school. I did one today, but it is lousy:

Adventure Acad
is fun

So be a pupil,
not a dum dum

Well, it is quite good rhyming. But I forgot to say anything about getting Daring Deed badges.

I 'spect Yeller is coming soon.

From your
Littly

Dear Mom and Dad,

Arrrroooo! the mailman came today with a big package. He said, "Phew, heavy, hint, hint." So I said to put the package down in the hall, and I filled up his hands with gold.

He said, "Gee thanks, Master L, you are a lot nicer than your Uncle Bigbad. When he was here being Head of Cunning College for Brute Beasts, he used to eat mailmen. He was a big horrible miser, he was. They say he had bags and bags of gold buried all over the place, but he never spent one penny, not like you. Good thing he went 'bang' if you ask me."

I gave him a small wolfly nip and a cheeky grrrr, and off he went, happy and rich.

All of a suddenly, the package went *crickle crackle rip!* Out jumped something saying a huge big RRRRRRRRRAAAAAAAAAHHHH! making my heart hop like frogs. And what was it? It was Yeller! I was so happy to see his funny pointy face and my trick arrow through his head. And it was so good to hear his voice again, yelling, "HELLO, LICKLE. HOW DID YOU LIKE MY TRICK PACKAGE?"

Who else would think of a clever trick joke like mailing yourself? Plus he brought me a present—a book for writing our adventures in. I am calling it My Diary of Daring Deeds, so 1 day all our grandcubs will read it and go, "Oooh look, so brave," etc.

Yours proudly,

 Little

ADVENTURE ACADEMY

FRETTNIN FOREST, BEASTSHIRE
HEADS: LITTLE WOLF AND YELLER WOLF, ESQS

Dear Mom and Dad,

I got your crool letter that says you will
not move in here with me. Whyo Y have you
changed your minds? Is it because Uncle
Bigbad went "bang" and Dad blames me?
I bet it is. But I told him not to eat all my
bakebeans with a shovel. He just did not
listen, being such a greedy guts.

PLEEEEEZ change your minds back again.

Yours upsettly,

Little

Dear Mom and Dad,

Murkshire is nice, yes, and the lair is cozy, yes. But you will soon like Beastshire when you see it. Also, Frettnin Forest is just the scaryest! Dad will love it.

But you say you think my plans are 2 showoffish and cubbish. Dad says he does not agree with Adventure Playgrounds. He is so oldfashy. When you are rich and modern, you can buy adventures and be daring deeders at home. No point to go a long way for them. See?

Yours pantingly,

Litlly

Dear M and D,

Just to show you what you are missing, look at this ad. Yeller found it in Wolf Weekly yesterday.

**MISTER MARVO'S
INSTANT ADVENTURES**
SCARY BUT SAFE
ALSO WINTERPROOF AND
UNBREAKABLE BY BRUTE BEASTS
DEMONSTRATIONS
BY APPOINTMENT

See? it is perfect. I am writing for a Mister Marvo appointment today! So come on, Mom and Dad, get on the helicopter quick!

Yours reallywantingly,

Littly

ᴀDVENTURE ᴀCADEMY

FRETTNIN FOREST, BEASTSHIRE
HEADS: LITTLE WOLF AND YELLER WOLF, ESQS

Dear Mom and Dad,

Yes, I was surprised when the helicopter landed and baby bro Smellybreff got out but not you. Yes, I got your note from him. No, he did not get sick on his new sailor suit.

Yes, I made sure he did not leave his bear in the helicopter. Yes, I do know Teddy is his best friend.

Yes, I do understand that you are trusting me with your small darling baby pet till Springtime comes. Yes, I know you will go RAVING MAD if I let anything bad happen to him.

Yes, I promise I will keep writing and say if Smellybreff gets homesick or bangs his tiny nose, etc.

Yes, you are right, it is furfluffingly chilly here, and all the chestnuts have fallen.

I hope you enjoy your long winter without us. Are you sure you do not want to have your tiny Smells with you, tucked up cozy in his bed?

Yours ??ly,

Little

Dear Mom and Dad,

Smells has been here 2 days now. He has been stupid and whiny, and he keeps messing my things up. Also, he will not call me and Yeller "sir," even if we are Heads.

He is hopeless at school and playing teacher. But 1 thing he likes a lot is gold. I bought him a metal detector yesterday, and he went off hunting for more of Uncle Bigbad's gold. He found 4 more bags, and now he wants a safe with a big key PLUS combination lock.

Yours fedupply,

Little

ADVENTURE ACADEMY

FRETTNIN FOREST, BEASTSHIRE
HEADS: LITTLE WOLF AND YELLER WOLF, ESQS

Dear Mom and Dad,

Guess what! A letter came from Mr. Marvo today. He is coming soonly to tell us all about Instant Adventures for our playground, arrroooo! Yeller has some brilliant BIG IDEAS for what we want: gokarts, motorbikes, roller-coasters, zipwire, dodgems, wall-of-death, helter skelter, parachute-jumper, arcade racing machines, etc! And what is so awful about that, Dad? Answer: nothing.

No naps for us cubs, because we are much 2 excited.

Yours can'twaitly,

L.

Dear Mom and Dad,

Smells wants me to send you a pic of his new safe, so here it is:

Also, he says har, har, he knows the number to open it, but not me. So cubbish.

Your big boy,

L.

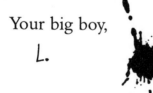

Dear Mom and Dad,

Smells is OK today, but a bit goldfeverish. He howled his head off till I gave him all my gold to put in his safe. Plus he keeps finding new bags with his metal detector.

This is what he does all the time. First he piles up gold in sixes (he only knows numbers up to 6). Then he kisses each pile and puts them in his safe. Then he locks up. Then he whispers to the coins inside the safe, "Night night, sleepy tight. Daddy will find you some more nice shiny friends to chink with."

What do you think about this?

Askingly,
Little Wolf

19

ADVENTURE ACADEMY

FRETTNIN FOREST, BEASTSHIRE
HEADS: LITTLE WOLF AND YELLER WOLF, ESQS

Dear Mom and Dad,

Just got your letter saying let Smells keep playing. Good, because I have.

From your not-so-wurrid

Little

Dear Mom and Dad,

Good thing Adventure Acad is snowproof. Outside it's all white, Yeller's worst thing. It made his voice lose some of its loudness. He said to me, "OH NO, NOW MISTER MARVO WON'T COME! THE SNOW IS TERRIBLE!"

But Mister Marvo did come—by snowmobile! It is a big shiny one with a propeller behind it, plus a cozy glass cab in front. Mister M. is tall and dashing with his black coat sticking out at the back and a big fuzzy beard. It comes right up to his glinty eyes. His voice is sleepy, and he smells like pepper, and his eyebrows are red and bristly.

After snacks Mister Marvo showed Yeller and me some plans of Instant Adventures. He does nice curly capitals, and he is a good color-inner. But plans are hard to understand for small cubs. Never mind, because Mister Marvo is so clever. He says, "Believe me, my boys, these are the most marvelous, most modernest adventures money can buy! They cost a lot, but remember, they are all under 1 winterproof dome. So you can have the thrills without the chills."

Yeller said, "ARRROOOO! BECAUSE SNOW IS MY WORST THING. IT GIVES ME THE TREMBLES. BUT GUESS WHAT, LICKLE? WE CAN HAVE A GO WITHOUT THE SNOW!!"

See what you are missing?

Yours xcitedly,

L.

Dear M and D,

Smells thinks Mister Marvo is brilliant. He has let him share his dorm. He has also shown him his ted and his safe, even!

Yeller and I are not jealous because now we can get on playing Bossy Heads and Daring Deeders by ourselves—important for the practiss. And tomorrow we choose our Instant Adventures. Arrroooo!

Yours thrilly,

ADVENTURE ACADEMY

FRETTNIN FOREST, BEASTSHIRE
HEADS: LITTLE WOLF AND YELLER WOLF, ESQS

Dear Mom and Dad,

Plan, plan, plan is what me and Yeller and Mister Marvo are up to. Phew! Smells will not help. He only likes counting gold.

These are our best IAs so far (short for Instant Adventures):

PIRATE RAIDERS

SPACE RANGERS

FIERCE FIGHTERS

NIGHT ON MONSTER MOUNTAIN

TARZAN ZIPWIRES

Mister Marvo asked did we want a BANGS-U-LIKE ADVENTURE, which is like a forest? You creep through it, and lots of pretend hunters jump out and shoot their play guns at you. Yeller said, "GOOD IDEA, I LOVE LOUDNESS."

But I said, "No, that is enough IAs for now."

I did not want to say I am very scared of bangs, but all of a suddenly, Mister Marvo said softly, "Look deep into my eyes, my boy, and tell me: Are bangs your worst thing?" Just then Yeller did a loud sneeze. Lucky for me! It made me jump, which kept me from giving away my secret.

So Mister Marvo said, "Well done, my boy. It is plain that you do not fear bangs. You are thinking of your pupils. They will not all be as fearless as you. By the way, the Instant Adventures you have selected will cost 3 wheelbarrowsful of gold, paid in advance."

I said, "What, before you build anything?
Good joke, har, har."

Mister Marvo got quite snarly then. It
made his beard slip a little. But quick as a
chick, he hid his sharp teeth. And now he
says he will build us a nice Example IA to
show us his marvelous work. Not the big
winterproof dome, because that goes on last.
No, it is a mini TARZAN ZIPWIRE. Good
one, huh?

Yours,

LitHy

Dear M and D,

Smells is still OK, but he's a little bit jealous and fidgety because Mister Marvo is doing planning with us. Yesterday Smells kept climbing on top of his safe and falling off, just so we would stick Band-Aids on him.

Then Yeller got a BIG IDEA. He made Smells a tape of gold going *chinkle chinkle*. Now it is 1 of his best things. He sits and listens to it all the time with his Walkwolf on.

See, we are looking after him.

Your trusted

Little

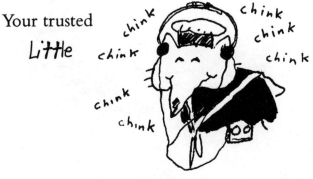

Dear Mom and Dad,

Today Mister Marvo put up the mini Tarzan Zipwire in our dorm to show us.

I asked Yeller, "Yeller, what do you think?" He said to me, "I THINK IT IS KIND OF SILLY, LICKLE." Mister Marvo said to Yeller, "With respect, my boy, Master Little is the true owner here. I advise you to keep silent." He gave Yeller a deep look in the eyes, and guess what? Yeller said, "OF COURSE, MISTER MARVO." It is so hard to say no to Mister Marvo.

True, the zipwire is smaller than we had hoped. It's more clothesliney than Tarzanny. But still, we had 236 turns on it. It is good the way it makes your eyes water and blows your fur back. Also, you go *dong!* off the tires at the end, and that takes some daringness.

Mister Marvo says not to be wurrid, because it is just an Example IA. When we pay him, he will build a huge, big, scary, real one over a stream with pretend crocs going *snap!*

Yours phewly,

L.

Adventure Academy

FRETTNIN FOREST, BEASTSHIRE
HEADS: LITTLE WOLF AND YELLER WOLF, ESQS

Dear Mom and Dad,

Sorry to hear about your blizzard blowing.
It's another white-whisker day here, too. So
stay tucked in, and see you in Springtime. We
cubs are much 2 busy for long zizzing.

Yes, I will write down all the news but not
send it. I'll just save it for Spring. I will put it
all in my Daring Deed book that Yeller gave
me. No, I will not disturb you—only in an
emerjuncy, like if any badness happens to my
baby bro, which it will not, Dad, because yes,
I do remember what you get like when you
go RAVING MAD.

Yours nightnightnightnightnightnightly, etc.,

L.

ADVENTURE ACADEMY
FRETTNIN FOREST, BEASTSHIRE
HEADS: LITTLE WOLF AND YELLER WOLF, ESQS

Dear Mom and Dad,

Mister Marvo is still here. He is doing lots of hard complications, and guess what he says? He says, "My boys, you now have my personal guarantee, as a marvoman and inventor, that your Instant Adventure Playground, the finest in the world, will be ready by the end of the month! My team of busy beavers will start work as soon as I give the word."

Arrroooo! Time to get our pupils together. I must think up a good school slogan.

Yours thinkingly,
Little

Dear M and D,

Smells has gone loony about Yeller's "chinkle" tape. He loves it, kiss, kiss! He has stopped talking to everybody. He only likes staying in his dorm guarding his safe, so that he can count his gold and listen to his chinkle tape on his Walkwolf.

I think Mister Marvo is a little upset. He keeps saying, "My boy, this won't do at all. Won't you look deep into my eyes and say, Yes, Mister Marvo, I am your best pal?" But Smells just turns up his Walkwolf and sings, "Chinkle chinkle little gold, you are what I like to hold."

Yours reportingly,

L. Wolf (Head)

Dear M and D,

Yeller has thought of a way for getting pupils. It is just the best! That is Y I am writing this in a balloon!!! It has the shape of Adventure Acad, but with a basket hanging underneath.

We are floating over Frettnin Forest. We have cardboard loudshouters, and this is what we shout (Yeller made it up but I wrote it down):

"Ahoy, ahoy, brute beasts!! Do you like adventures? Then come to our school and have some. Yes, come to Adventure Academy! It is the big place they used to call Cunning College. Mister Bigbad Wolf was the Head. But not anymore. He went BANG and died. So all is changed, and no need to fear and fret. Little and Yeller Wolf are the new Heads. So come, be our pupils! Try our new adventure playground. It is the BEST FUN EVER! Plus, you get Daring Deed Awards. Arrroooo!"

Yours skyhighly,

L.

ADVENTURE ACADEMY

FRETTNIN FOREST, BEASTSHIRE
HEADS: LITTLE WOLF AND YELLER WOLF, ESQS

Dear Mom and Dad,

I'm a little bit wurrid about baby bro again. It is gold, gold, gold all the time with him now.

I know you think he doesn't have goldfever. But last night he gave his precious ted a bath in gold! I am afraid he is a little bit gone in the brane, because everybody knows Smells hates baths.

Also, he has locked Mister Marvo out of his dorm and will not speak to him at all.

Yours ohwelly,

Little

Adventure Academy

FRETTNIN FOREST, BEASTSHIRE
HEADS: LITTLE WOLF AND YELLER WOLF, ESQS

Dear Parents,

Good news! Our balloon ad worked.
Now we have 1 pupil. He was left on our
doorstep. He is a small crow with not many
feathers, very shy, and with a label tied on
him. He does not say much, only "Ark." This
is what the label said:

> STUBBS CROW
> TOO AFRAID TO FLY
> BUT GOOD AT
> BEAKWORK

Yours,

L. Wolf (Head)

Adventure Academy

FRETTNIN FOREST, BEASTSHIRE
HEADS: LITTLE WOLF AND YELLER WOLF, ESQS

Dear Parents,

Some cubs would look at Stubbs and say, "Hmm, nice snack," but not me and Yeller. We want to teach him, not eat him.

Yeller is good at being a Head. He shouts cheery things like, "HELLO, STUBBY! WELCOME TO ADVENTURE ACADEMY. I AND MY CO-HEAD LICKLE WILL SOON TEACH YOU HOW TO BE A HIGH FLYER AND DARING DEEDER LIKE US. BEAK UP! NO NEED TO BE A SCAREDYCROW!"

Also, we have let Stubbs nest in the fireplace in the hall with his head up the chimney to feel at home.

Yours Headly,

L.

ADVENTURE ACADEMY
FRETTNIN FOREST, BEASTSHIRE
HEADS: LITTLE WOLF AND YELLER WOLF, ESQS

Dear Parents,

Mister Marvo has finished with his complications, and he keeps asking and asking us for 1 wheelbarrowful of gold at least—just to start up, he says. It is hard saying no to him, but Yeller says we must try and keep our firmness up, saying, "NO MEANS NO!" with loud grrrs like Dad.

If Mister M. asks me, what I do is cross my eyes and go "blah doo dum diddle" in my head.

I just heard him going *mumblymumbly* up to bed. I wish he would hurry up and bring his busy beavers to start work on the Adventure Playground. Then he can have his gold.

Yours keentostartly,

L.

ADVENTURE ACADEMY
FRETTNIN FOREST, BEASTSHIRE
HEADS: LITTLE WOLF AND YELLER WOLF, ESQS

Morning

Dear Mom and Dad,

Good thing I am writing this in my Diary of Daring Deeds and not mailing this yet. Because I think you might get a little bit mad.

It is just that Mister Marvo has stolen all my gold and cubnapped Smells. Sorry!

Your other boy,

L Wolf

P.S. Please do not get wurrid. By the time you read this, everything will be OK. Probly.

ADVENTURE ACADEMY

FRETTNIN FOREST, BEASTSHIRE
HEADS: LITTLE WOLF AND YELLER WOLF, ESQS

Later

Dear Mom and Dad,

Help, we do not know what to do! Because
1) the snow is as tall as cubs, and 2) Yeller is
scared of snow. How can we catch up to Mister
Marvo in his fast snowmobile? Ooo-er!

Just back from a clue hunt. Near the front
door we found:

1 top hat

1 bushy beard

1 long coat with red
tailhairs all up the back inside.

What do they mean?

Yours stumpedly,

Little

Much later

Dear M and D,

Oh no. Guess what? Mister Marvo is not really a marvoman and inventor at all! No, he is a cunning fox and a clever dizgizzer (cannot spell it). And his really truly name is Mister Twister the Fox! He was Uncle Bigbad's crime partner, remember? Also, he made me work for him at Borderlands Market 1 time when I was lost. Imagine me not knowing him by his pepper smell, plus his sneaky questions, like are bangs my worst thing? plus his saying MY BOY THIS and MY BOY THAT all the time!

WANTED

Mr. Twister (Fox)

HUGE REWARD

Smells left a clue too, but it is no good because he can't write any letters after ABC. This is the clue:

Do not fret and fear, though. I 'spect Yeller will think up a rescue idea soon.

Yours onyourmarksly,

Little

Middle of Frettnin Forest
(small gap in)

Dear M and D,

The cheery news is we are on the trail of
Mister Twister on my bike (Yeller's idea—
quicker than paws). He has got the
snowtrembles very bad. His voice has gone
all quiet. This morning he whispered to me,
"LICKLE, THE SNOW HAS TOOK MY VOICE."

I said, "Yeller, that is an old wolf's tale.
The snow does not want voices." He is still
wurrid, but he will not let me go on my
ownly. Also, Stubbs did not want to stay
behind, so we tucked him in our knapsack.
With his head sticking out, it is a little bit
like flying for him, only not 2 high up.

We have plenty of snacks, a tent, flashlights, etc. Also, Yeller brought Smells's clue, plus his kite with the yellow wolf eyes and strong string as a Rescue Kit. Now we are having a short rest in a small gap in Frettnin Forest. Two cold stars are lighting this letter, maybe 3. Brrr! I think we have come 4 or 5 miles. If we keep on the snowmobile track, fine. If not, *whoops,* plop! Where are we? Answer: under the snow, digging.

Yours searchingly,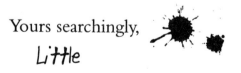

Little

P.S. We will rescue Smells as quick as we can, so do not go RAVING MAD.

Dear Mom and Dad,

What a rooty nightride we had through Frettnin Forest! The tent was so heavy on the back of the bike, and it pressed on the brakes and made us go even slower. But all is not sadness and sore bottoms, because we have reached the south shore of Lake Lemming. Now it is very late, but we can rest. The tent is up and it's a snuggly fit with 3 of us in it.

Yeller and me had hedgehog and parsley soup for a warmup. I said to Stubbs, "Do crows like chocklit earwigs?" He said "Ark! Ark-zactly!" his 1st words. He is a bit shy for Rescue work.

Yours sorebottomly,

L.

45

Dear Mom and Dad,

I cannot sleep because of thinking: Y did Mister Twister take Smells with him? Is it...

A) because he likes small pests, or

B) because Smells loves gold so much he will not say the combination of the safe?

I bet it is B. And I bet when they are far away, Mister Twister will take the Walkwolf off Smells's ears. Then he will say softly, "Look deep into my eyes, my boy, and tell me the numbers of your safe." Not fair, because Mister Twister is such a cunning crook and cubnapper, but Dad will still go raving mad at me for letting a bad thing happen to Smells.

Your grumpy

Little

Dear Mom and Dad,

Yeller and me were all down and dumpy after only a small zizz. I was on the back of the bike because it was Yeller's turn to pedal. He said whisperly, "PHEW, LICKLE, THIS IS 2 HARD FOR ME. I WISH THERE WAS A MORE EASY WAY TO CATCH THAT SNOWMOBILE."

Just then Stubbs tapped me on the head and pointed his beak northly. I said, "Do you mean go straightly, the crow way?" He said, "Ark." I said, "But that is straight over the lake." He said, "Ark-zactly!"

But we didn't know how to cross the hard ice lid on the lake, which was 2 skiddy for bikers. Then I said, "Wait, the plastic picnic plates!"

We got off the bike, and Yeller and me
tied 1 plate on each back paw. Then onto the
lake we stepped. "Hold tight, Stubbs!" I said,
and off we went, skaty skate! 1st we went:
FFFSHH-BONK, OOO, MY NOSE!
FFFSHH-BONK, OOO, MY TAIL!

But then Stubby spread out his wings for
balance, and off we sailed, smooth as smooth!
That gave Yeller the idea to use his kite, so
no more falling down for us. Oooh, what a
thrilly feeling, and FREE! Better than silly old

Tarzan Zipwires that cost wheelbarrowsful of money! Also, a good Daring Deed for my Diary, check. ✔

1 bad thing about picnic plates is they are brakeless, so we met the north shore in a sudden way. Lucky for us, there was a soft snowpile to land in. Phew!

We brushed ourselves off, and guess what we saw right away? Snowmobile tracks going hillward. Arrroooo! So that Mister Twister had better watch out! We know he has gone to Windy Ridge!

Yours Sherlockly,

Little

P.S. Also, we found a small pile of gray fluffy stuff. Not sure what it is, but Stubbs kept it for a cozy nest liner.

Dear Mom and Dad,

After a short rest, we all did jumping up and down for the warmness. Also, we made a fire for toasting cheese (Stubbs's best snack). A crunchy shrewbar for Yeller and me, then we went back to doing Rescuing.

All afternoon we hiked pantingly. At last Stubbs tapped my head, and then his beak pointed over the hill to Windy Ridge. Aha! There was the snowmobile, with Mister Twister plus Smells tied up! Yeller said (small trembly voice), "LET'S CREEP UP CLOSE, THEN WAIT FOR DEEP DARK. THEN WE CAN JUMP ON THAT FOX AND CAPTURE HIM!"

We got on our belly fur in the cold snow, doing the wolf crawl. Poor Yeller! It was so bad for his snowtrembles. But Stubbs helped

50

him keep up his cheeryness, whispering, "Ark! Ark-cellent! Ark-cellent!" all the way to the top.

We waited and waited, quiet as cat's breath, till the dark was deep. Then, one paw at a time, careful not to make the snow squeak:

We got out our flashlights,

and we snuck up behind Mister Twister,

and we tied him up quick!

Only it was not Mister Twister! It was only a cardboard cutout and a note:

My boys, you can never hope to catch me. It is only a matter of time before the brat tells me the combination for the safe. Then I shall release him. So give up and go home. Otherwise, you will put the brat in danger and you will face some VERY LOUD BANGS. You have been warned. Give up now, signed Mister Twister.

Yours trickedly,

Little

Dear Mom and Dad,

Today was just the worst. Mister Twister had tons of time to escape across the Dark Hills plus get here to Broken Tooth Caves.

Before we started, Yeller said, "BANGS ARE YOUR WORST THING, LICKLE. DO YOU WANT TO GIVE UP?" I said, "Snow is your worst thing. Do you want to give up?" We both said, "No!" and kept going. So now Mister Twister will most probly join up with some outlaws in a gang and bash us.

The Dark Hills were very cold and horrible with snow coming down. So, no more snowmobile tracks. Then that sharp stuff, not snow, flew down. Is it called sleet?

This is a bad place. So many caves, all joined together like rat runs. Just the lurky sort that outlaws and bears like. Ooo-er!

We have picked a good dry cave for our night lair. Hope we can keep safe.

Your tracky boy,

Little

Dear Mom and Dad,

Today we did a Daring Deed with a lion in it. Yes, a real mountain kind!

We slept a safe night, but boiling up bat soup for breakfast was 2 much of a danger-tempter, because a hungry old mountain lion came sniffing! Stubbs smelled its catsmell even before me, and he saved us from ambush. He went, "Ark! Ark-shun! Ark-shun stations!" We just had time to run behind the fire. All of a suddenly, we saw the lion's eyes, then his teeth, then his blue cap and jacket. He went:

OOOO ARRRR OOOO ARRRRR O GGGG OO GRRRRA AAAAA AAAHHHH HHHH

Stubbs whispered, "Ark! Ark-zaggerating," which I did not think so, because my ears were ringing. But Stubbs flapped his short wings at the fire and puffed up the flames and smoke. And do you know what? That lion was not as fierce as his roar. Because he started coughing and crept away!

Then he tried to trick us with big stories. He said, "Oy be a narsty ole RRRRobber ye know. And oy be a wicked ole RRRRRipper!"

Quick as a chick, I said, "Listen, Mister Mountainlion. If you help us, maybe we can find a nice juicy mice pie or 3 for you, yes?"

No more snarls at all after that—just chew, chew, lipsmack, lipsmack.

That is how we craftily found out these things:

1) a fox and small wolf cub stayed in a secret hideout cave last night

2) that same fox went HAR, HAR about trick cutouts

3) that same fox said he was going to learn his map by heart and chew it up so nobody could follow

4) that same fox said to the small wolf cub about going across the border into Grimshire, to Hamneezia, the forgotten village.

Now can you guess who that fox and wolf cub are!!?

Yours aharly,

Little

Dear Mom and Dad,

Stubbs woke us up today going, "Ark! Ark-shun stations!" He was having a nightmare about getting lost. That made me get wurrid because of not having a map. But then I said, "Quick, Yeller, give me the string from your kite. We are off to find the secret hideout cave where Mister Twister and Smells spent the night!"

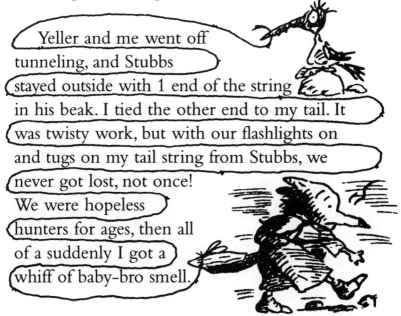

Yeller and me went off tunneling, and Stubbs stayed outside with 1 end of the string in his beak. I tied the other end to my tail. It was twisty work, but with our flashlights on and tugs on my tail string from Stubbs, we never got lost, not once! We were hopeless hunters for ages, then all of a suddenly I got a whiff of baby-bro smell.

"Arrroooo," I said. "This is it, the secret hideout cave!"

Yeller said, "YOU'RE RIGHT, LICKLE, BECAUSE LOOK—BITS OF CHEWED MAP ALL OVER THE FLOOR!"

Just then I saw another clue. It was some more of that gray fluffy stuff like we found by Lake Lemming! We picked up the paper and the fluff, then I went *tug tug* on the string, and Stubbs pulled me in like a fish. Outside in the daytime light I said, "Oh boo, this is not like maps. It's more like spilled ratflakes. Now we will never find the way."

Stubbs said, "Ark! Ark-zammin! Ark-zammin!" meaning, Let me see. He tucked the fluff in with his other nest liner in the knapsack. Then we found out why his label said he was good at beakwork. Because

he got all the chewed-up bits of paper and stuck them together with spider webs. So, arrroooo, we are mapless no more!

Northeast is the quick way to Hamneezia from here. Too bad it is over the Grim Mountains—they are a bit 2 high for small crows scared of highness. Still, Stubbs says he will go for the Arksperience. Brave, huh? Hope he does not get 2 dizzy.

Yours readysteadyly,

Little

Dear Mom and Dad,

We were off early, with Stubbs snuggled down in the gray fluffy stuff at the bottom of my knapsack. Three Grim Mountains ago I said to Yeller, "I hate this high land. It is 2 hard on paws."

But we went struggling up Mount Tester. It was slippy, but then we found new tricks for climbing. Stubbs kept saying muffly, "Ark! Ark-cellent," meaning, "Well done." Mount Tester was a hard tester for climbing (get it?), hard up the south side, hard down the north side.

Then came Mount Skyward, about the same. But halfway up Mount Farview, it got 2 steep. The cliff started leaning out over us! I was nearly keeping up with Yeller, but all of a suddenly I lost my pull. I could not go up and I could not go down. My trembles made Stubbs pop out to look. I said, "No, Stubbs! It's 2 high up for you! Stay inside the knapsack!"

But he would not. He struggled out, saying, "Arks Arks!"

I said, "Ice axe? Where?" and he gave me a small peck on the head. I said, "Your beak?" And that was what he meant.

So I took a trusting hold of his twiggy legs, and UP I swung him. Then I gave a loud arrrooooo for the best beak I know, because it stuck in the ice like a bee's stinger in a bear's nose!

And that was how Yeller, Stubbs, and me climbed the highest, harshest mountain in Beastshire. All on our ownly, we would be dead now. But together, slow but sure, we have done a Daring Deed like no cub or crowlet has ever done before. So into the Diary of Daring Deeds it goes, check. ✓

Now we are the high-uppest campers in Beastshire.

Yours daringly,

L. Wolf

Hamneezia,
Grimshire

Dear Mom and Dad,

Which do you think was our worst:
climbing down from Mount Farview, or
crossing the rope bridge over Perilus Pass?
Answer: the bridge, because mountains are
cold and crool, but they do not wobble. Also,
rope bridges try to tip you—AHHHEEEeeee
splosh!—into roary water with sharp rocks
sticking up. So that is enough writing about
Perilus Bridge, which was as bad as bangs,
nearly.

So I will tell you about Hamneezia. We got
here after dark with snow floating down, very
frozz and gloomy and glum. Nobody here
remembers a snowmobile coming through. All
the natives of Hamneezia just forget
everything.

Yours brrrly,

L.

Dear M and D,

That Hamneezia was bad for our branes! It made us feel giveuppish. So we ran off quick the next day. Now we are in Spooke, where the silver miners live. It is nice if you like old huts and piles of rubble everywhere.

There is 1 good game they have here in Spooke. It is called Hello Ween, and it goes like this. 1st you must have some gloomyness and pumpkins with candles in them. Yum, tasty! Next, you dress up like a witch or ghosty or skerlington (cannot spell it). Then you walk up and down the street going *woo!* Then you go up to a door, *knock knock.* Then you say, "TREACLE TRICK!!" And you are given yummy snacks to eat!

Yeller said, "HEY, LICKLE, OUR PUPILS WILL LOVE THIS! LET'S BUY SOME BOOGIEBEAST MASKS WITH GREEN GLOWPAINT ON THEM. THEN WE CAN TEACH HELLO WEEN AT ADVENTURE ACADEMY." So we bought lots of them.

Tonight we are having a nice cozy curl-up. We want to get our strongness up for rescuing Smells.

3 woos from

Little

woo WOO WOO

Dear M and D,

Oh no! Yeller is in bed with his tremblyest Snowtrembles ever! Here is the story of Y.

We were asking and asking in Spooke for clues about Mister Twister, but in a hopeless way. Then—nice surprise—we came to Bodger Badger's Garage and met a cheery badger working there. I said, "Have you seen a snowmobile, a big shiny one with a propeller behind it?"

The badger said, "Oooh, arr. Lemmy see. Oooh, arr. Snowmobile? Yerss, me dears. Stopped by here 3 days ago, oooh, arr.  Nice lady driving there was. Her hair was whyte as snow. She asked me to put on an extra big fuel tank, yerss she did. And she bought an extra-strong roof rack and all. She had this big heavy iron box, oooh, arr. That took up too much room in the cab, you see?"

Stubbs said, "Ark! Ark-straordinary!"

I said, "Was there a small, smelly wolf cub with this old lady?"

The badger said, "Dunno about no wolf cub, oooh, arr. She had her baby grandson with her, but I never did see his face. Poor thing—he had the chickypox. So his granny had to wrap him up tight all over ter keep him from scratchin', see? Looked like a little Egyptian mummy he did, oooh, arr."

I said, "But was he very squeaky and wiggly?"

The badger said, "Oooh, arr! Ever so squeaky and wiggly!"

I said, "I think I know that squeaky baby. And did the old lady smell like pepper, by any chance?"

Answer: "OOOH, ARR!! Yerss!"

"AND WHICH WAY DID THEY GO?" asked Yeller.

Answer: northeast toward Yellowsmoke. "But oooh, arr, you don't want to go there on foot, me dears," said the badger. "Not across the White Wildness. There be no roads to follow, you know, nor no shelter. Just blizzards brewing. The worstest, snowyest place on earth, that is."

That was when Yeller fainted. Now he is tucked up tight in Bodger Badger's spare room. Maybe he will feel better tomorrow.

Yours let'shopingly,

L. Wolf

Dear Mom and Dad,

Stubbs and me have gone on alone. We miss Yeller a lot. But he was 2 ill to come with us. Also, he feels much shame to be a giverupper.

But I said, "Never mind, Yeller, some beasts do not like high places, and some beasts do not like bangs. You WISH you were just normal and untrembly, but you are not, so there."

I am writing sadly in a snowhole in the White Wildness. It is true what they say about the whiteness—it is all white here, even the bears.

So no more now from

Little Wolf

Dear Mom and Dad,

Brrrrrr. So frozz, so weak.

Stubbs says all crows are Arksperts on going the quick way. That is why everybody says, "It is 2 miles as the crow flies, etc." Except Stubbs of course—he hates flying. Anyway, he says we are going northeast.

But I am not so sure. I have run and run today. But Yellowsmoke is not near.

I have dug a snow cave.

2 cold 2 write more,

L.

snowcave,
white wildness

Dear M and d,

So tired   sore eyes   blizzard bad
trapped in snowcave

no food today   just lick snow   zizz   wake

sometimes I send up my Emerjuncy
Howl for the wind to carry

But I am getting 2 weak

we have put out Yeller's kite to fly for a
signal Also Stubbs has braided the string for
strongness

the wolfeyes on it shine   but who will see?

From
L W

drear mumdad, I cannot stay wakey only

dream of monster big growler

coming   closer   closer

Dear Mom and Dad,

Phew! It's days since I wrote to you.
Sorry—it was the weakness.

About my dream: It was not a dream. It was
the Snowmonster who crawled into our snow
cave to take us away. Shiny blue body, blue head,
and buggy eyes—he was a terror, but he came
whisperingly. He did not roar. Do you know Y?

Because he was not the Snowmonster.
He was YELLER!!

He was wearing Bodger Badger's blue
snowsuit! Off came his helmet and goggles
and earmuffs. And there was his funny, pointy
face and his stickyout teeth,
laughing. His voice is still
not back to normal
loudness, but even
whispery it makes you

laugh. He said, "SORRY TO KEEP YOU WAITIN'.
ANYBODY WANNA NICE FIGHT?"

I said ME! and over and over we rolled,
the happiest wrestlers ever! It was too hot
and squashy for small crows, but soon Stubbs
forgot his shyness and joined in with some
good rough pecks. That night we had a
newsy Togetheragain Feast with yummy stuff
from Bodger's pantry. Rabbit rolls and mice
pies for me and Yeller—mmm, yes, please!
And Stubbs had his faves—worms on toast
and crawlycake.

I will tell Yeller's news next time.

Yours togetherly,

Dear M and D,

Here is Yeller's story. He told it like this.

"WELL, LICKLE AND STUBBY, THAT TIME YOU
WEN' AWAY, I FELT SHOCK AN' I FELT SHAME. I FELT
THE LONEST WOLF CUB IN THE LAND. I KEPT
THINKIN', 'I MUST HELP MY CHUMS.' BUT EVERY
TIME I GOT OUT OF BED, I THOUGHT OF THE
WHITE WILDNESS. AND I JUST FELL ON MY FACE,
FLOP—LIKE THAT! I COULDN'T STOP FAINTIN', NOT
WITH THE TREMBLES SO SHOCKIN'.

"THEN ONE LONE NIGHT, I HEARD SOMETHIN'
CALLIN' ME. IT WAS COMIN' DOWN MISTER
BODGER'S CHIMNEY—FARAWAY LIKE, BUT STILL
CLEAR AS WATER. I SAYS TO MYSELF, "THAT'S
LICKLE'S EMERJUNCY HOWL, THAT IS! HE WOULDN'T
USE THAT IF HE WASN'T IN A DREADFUL BAD WAY!'
SO UP I JUMPS, CALLING, 'MISTER BODGER, MISTER
BODGER! YOU'VE GOT TO HELP ME SAVE MY CUZ
AND STUBBY CROW FROM DEATH BY BLIZZARDS!'

"HE SAYS TO ME, 'ARE YOU UP TO IT?' I SAYS, 'I'VE GOT TO BE!'

"SO DOWN WE WENT TO THE GARAGE. MISTER BODGER GOT A BIG OLD MOTORBIKE, PLUS A BIG WHEEL OFF OF A TRACTOR, PLUS A SLED, AND HE JOINED 'EM ALL UP TOGETHER WITH SOME TOOLS. AND BEFORE MORNING CAME, HE MADE ME A SPEEDY SNOWTORBIKE! THEN HE GAVE ME HIS OLD BLUE SNOWSUIT AND GOGGLES—A BIT BIG FOR ME, BUT GOOD FOR GETTIN' MY BRAVENESS UP."

I said, "But still, how could you follow us? Our tracks were covered up quick! So how?"

"Ark! Arksplain!" said Stubbs.

Yeller said, "IT WAS THAT CLEVER CLUE FROM SMELLS!!"

I said, "Clever? Do you mean that screwed-up paper with the wobbly C, plus a splotch, plus yellow scribbles, like this?"

"WELL, LICKLE," said Yeller, "I FOUND OUT IT WAS NOT JUST SMELLS'S NORMAL DUNCENESS. NO, IT WAS A CRAFTY CLUE, MEANING:

C (SEE) YELLOW SMOKE!!"

So Yellowsmoke Swamplands is what Yeller aimed his snowtorbike at. And true, the snow was a terror to him, but he made the engine roar back at the blizzard. And at last he saw wolf eyes shining in the sky, and he thought, "I KNOW THAT KITE. I WILL SEE WHO IS ON THE END OF THE STRING!"

And he looked. And it was us. The end.
Another Daring Deed for my book! ✔
Arroooo!

Yours savedly,

L.

P.S. Now we can rescue Smells.
Let's hope he is still ok, huh?

Dear Mom and Dad,

Fast riding makes you say to walkers,
"You are just a slow snail!" But oh, for a
snowsuit plus a wooly hat to warm up my
cold ears!

Stubbs has his gray fluffy stuff in the
knapsack for cozyness. But I had to sit
behind Yeller and hold tight. We speeded
SWISHSWOOSH over snowbumps and
cracks. We went so quick that now the
Shivery Sea is just a short twinkling away.
Going WAAAAAH! was a big help. But not
having a wooly hat, my
face soon got frozz and
my WAAAAAH! got
stuck. When we
stopped, I could not
move. My mouth
looked like a mailbox
for polar bears.

Lucky they have hot steamers in this land, which are like yellow smoke coming up out of the ground. Yeller and Stubbs had to lift me off the snowtorbike seat like a cardboard cutout and sit me in a steamer. Phew! Goodbye, frozz, hello, warmalloverness! Plus, my mouth went yum, yum again for eating practiss!

We are camping here tonight. Do not get wurrid. We will soon capture Mister Twister and get Smells back, boo, shame. (Only kidding—I miss him, really.)

Yours,

Dear M and D,

Ooo-er! Hot steamers are a danger when they get as big as trees. We had to go along a wiggly path to miss them, and it was a hard 1 to stay on. So Yeller drove slow, and Stubbs and me were sharp lookouts. But sometimes we missed the path. Then, *whooosh!*— up we went like a Ping-Pong ball on a waterjet, and *bonk!*— down we went in the squishy mud. No wonder flying is scary for Stubbs.

At last we have found the Shivery Sea. Phew! It is gray and cold, like a big lake but more wavy. Plus it has pointy blue ice islands floating in it. We went up northly along the beach, searching, searching.

But not 1 clue about Mister Twister. Boo, shame.

Yours,

L.

80

Dear M and D,

We went south again by snowtorbike along the beach. The snow stopped, but still no foxy tracks.

But clever old Stubbs spotted some gray fluffy stuff, then some more, and some more! It led to a rowboat full of holes. And in the sand, right next to the rowboat, was a BIG boatprint, plus scrape marks going down to the sea.

Yeller looked on the floor of the rowboat. "OH NO!" he whispered. "SHOCKIN'!" His fur was standing up on his neck, because lying there, flat like a cowpat, was a small body.

All I could say was, "Gulp."

Yours dreadly,

Little

Dear M and D,

Good news! That cowpat was not Smells! It was his ted with all the stuffing pulled out.

I am so proud of my baby bro, even if he is a moany little miser. Unpicking his bear and dropping piles of stuffing out of it for us to follow was a wolfly thing to do. Foxes think they know all the best tricks, so har, har, Mister Twister, you never thought of that 1!

We spent today being boat fixers, maybe for a nice shelter. Also, we had a good chat, so now we think we know where Mister Twister has gone with Smells.

Yeller said, "I THINK MISTER TWISTER HAD A BIG BOAT HERE—BIG ENOUGH FOR A SNOWMOBILE PLUS A SAFE, LICKLE. AND NOW HE HAS GONE SAILIN' THE SHIVERY SEA."

But where xactly? Together we made a strong new skin for the boat, with flattened-out mud guards plus sled pieces off the snowtorbike. We buried the other parts. Also, we made oars out of tent poles and picnic plates. Yeller's kite makes a hansum sail.

Your fixy boy,

L.

P.S. Some crawly things just came sideways out of the sea and tried to pinch us with their pinchers. Handy, because it was snack time, yum, yum. 2 much salt on them, but nice and crunchy.

83

Dear M and D,

Today we lunched(?) lawnched(?) the boat.

We pushed it in the water (brrr, frozz!), so we crossed our toes for not sinking. It floated! I said, "You say a name for this boat, Stubbs." So Stubbs gave it the name "Ark"— just the thing.

Sailing Ark was very scary—a bit 2 hilly for wolf cubs. But not for Stubbs. He stood on the pointy part at the front of the boat, being the captain. Ups and downs did not bother him. I think it is a little bit like flying, but safe. His feathers are more bendy and black now, also shiny.

Yeller and me rowed fast to take our minds off the queezys. That puffed us out quick! Then silently, up popped some nice nosy sea creatures. Seals was their name. Have you heard of them? We said our names 2, and we told them that we were hunting for a cubnapper.

One of the seals barked up, "Well mateys, all hands on deck and hoist your mainsail! Because we spied a big boat 4 tides ago. She was bound for Vile Isle."

"Vile Isle?" I said.

"Ark! Arksplain!" said Stubbs.

"That's easy, me hearties," said the seal. "Vile Isle is bang in the middle of the Shivery Sea."

Now the seals are giving us a tow, so must stop, 2 joggy 2 write.

Your queezy boy, Little

P.S. Just a short riddle: What makes Yeller green? Answer: Blue. Also boats. (Hard 1, huh?)

Dear Mom and Dad,

Dry land—I love it, kiss, kiss, even if it is all boring rocks!

The seals towed us all the way here. On the way, we skimmed past lots of blue ice islands (seals call them ice burglars—I do not know Y). They were all jumpy with penguins.

At last we saw Vile Island. It is sort of a big black pile of rocks with a castle on top. And now we are on it (the island, not the castle). So 1 more Daring Deed for my book, check. ✔

Now I will tell you a proud thing about Smells. Yeller says he has been thinking about my small bro's clue. It was a much more crafty 1 than we thought before.

Do you remember that wobbly C with the yellow smudges next to it like this?

Well, it was not a wobbly C. It was a SHIVERY SEA! Get it?!! It was a small clue with a BIG meaning like this:

"Mister Twister is taking me to Vile Island next to the Yellowsmoke Swamplands in the middle of the Shivery Sea!"

Who would think a small brane like Smells's has got room for paper clues PLUS trails of bearstuffing? I must stop now. Yeller has thought of an idea for getting inside the castle. Now we can really start rescuing!

Yours herewegoly,

L.

Small brane

Dear M and D,

We have found Smells, but we have been sort of, um, trapped everlastingly.

One good thing yesterday was a new word I learned: "dungeons." Dungeons are what you fall into when you go creeping around in castles and go through trap doors. Otherwise my news is not much. We have been foiled by that foul, foxy tricker. Boo, grrr.

We were all going "ow" and rubbing our bottoms, then all of a suddenly, down came a peppery smell. We looked up, and way up above us, sharp eyes were looking down shiningly through the trap door. Next came a soft foxy chuckle and these words: "Good evening, my boys. Congratulations. I underestimated you. No one has ever found my secret hideout before. And now, welcome to my deepest, darkest dungeon.

Please pay attention while I gloat."

"You see, my boys, you have fallen quite literally into my trap. You can never escape. Smellybreff has proved, shall we say, difficult? My softest voice is wasted on him, and he is too fond of gold to give in to rough threats. So now it is up to you, my boys. Either persuade the little brat to give me the combination of the safe, or you will remain here forever. Here he comes now. Do try to talk some sense into him, won't you?"

A cat basket came down dangling. Smells was inside with a gag on.

Then BANG went the trap door! Just to make me tremble, I bet.

Your shaky boy,

L.

Dear Mom and Dad,

Still trapped everlastingly, boo, shame, and Mister Twister has pulled Smells up from the dungeons again. We just had time to say praising things like, "Good clues, Smells, you are a Daring Deeder, keep chinnupply, keep saying nothing." Then he was gone again, going mmmm, mmmm through his gag.

One problem. If Smells keeps saying nothing about combinations, Mister Twister will get his temper up, I bet. Good thing you are not here while these shocking adventures are happening to Smells and me.

L.

P.S. By the way, Stubbs wants me to write that he is holding my flashlight while I am doing this writing. So thanks, Stubbs. Nice beakwork.

Dear Mom and Dad,

Mister Twister came back to speak to us this morning, but not with his temper up. Phew! He only wanted to give us a  good-bye gloat. Boo, grrr. He says he has found a new way to make Smells be his friend again!

Because last night he told Smells a whopping fib—that he will let him be King of Beastshire! He says he can be on TV a lot, and all his subjects must give him their gold to put in his safe. Adventure Acad can be his palace, and he can wear a twinkly crown and boss everybody around, even me and Yeller.

That fox is such a tempter. Now Smells will tell him the combination, I bet!

And we will be in the dungeons forevermore.

Yours howlingly,

L.

Dear M and D,

We just heard Mister Twister's boat leaving. Oh no! We tracked him all this way to save Smells, and now we must get back quick to Adventure Acad to save him. But how?

What shall I do? My emerjuncy howl will not reach you at the lair. Plus, no mailbox near! How can I get to you? Now who will go RAVING MAD at Mister Twister and save Smells from his power? How can we ever escape from this deep, dark dungeon???

Wait—Yeller has just looked at me thinkingly. Quick, I must give him my pencil. Cross your toes he has an idea that wants writing down.

Yours rushingly,

L.

Vile Island, by the sea

Dear Mom and Dad,

Arrroooo! Yeller's idea was an escaping 1! So here is the story of the Daring Deed that got us out of the dungeons, a good 1 for my diary, check.

Yeller said, "QUICK, STUBBY, STAND ON LICKLE'S HEAD. GOOD. NOW, LICKLE, STAND ON MY HEAD. THAT'S IT. NOW STUBBY, TIME FOR SOME CLEVER BEAKWORK. TRY PICKIN' THE LOCK ON THE TRAP DOOR!"

Stubbs fainted 2 times because of highness, but otherwise it was easy peasy. The next hard part was climbing out, but *arrroooo* again for the Rescue Kit kite string—so handy!!

Off we went quick down to the seashore. But we were too late. That nasty Mister Twister had burned our boat!

Your macarooned boy,

L. B. Wolf

Dear M and D,

Just a quick note, but you will think, hmmm—interesting!

Being macarooned on Vile Island, we thought, well, what do rocky islands have for snacks? So we hunted in the rock pool, and we caught tickly swimming things like small commas with whiskers. They are very tasty. We also found chewy stars and the flat crunchy things with pinchers we tried before—lots of those. Plus we liked the clingy things that tuck up in their shells. Lucky Stubbs, having a beak—much quicker than noses.

Then something happened, like howling, but shivery and strange. Yeller found a broken drainpipe. He put 1 end into the water and said, "LICKLE, STUBBY. LISTEN DOWN THIS." The sound was sea creatures calling. I put my mouth to the pipe and called ARRROooOOOOOOoo!

Back came a call: AYEEEEEEEOOOEE.

What can it be?

L.

Dear M and D,

Today I arrroooooed down the pipe again, and guess what? All of a suddenly, black islands grew in the sea—12, maybe more. They spouted water like Yellowsmoke steamers!

Then they swam right up to us in a pack. The leader put his wide, flat chin on our beach and spoke softly. "Who calls for a ride across the whale road?" His mouth was big enough to swallow a snowmobile.

"D-d-do you mean a ride across the sea?" I said all trembly.

"That is not the whale name. To us it is the whale road," said the pack leader. "Our backs are at your service."

Down came his mighty tail for us, like a ramp. The other whales made a line in front of him. Stubbs hopped into my knapsack, and Yeller gave a nod. Then off we went across the whale road, running, running, till we crossed the Shivery Sea and reached the shore of Grimshire.

Yours puffed-outly,

L.

P.S. Big ✔ for a brilliant DD!

Dear M and D,

Still puffed out today, and now we are camping yawnly not far from the River Riggly.

Whale road running was hard yesterday, and so was quickmarching southly today. But we must save Smells—he does not know what a tricker that fox is! So come on, Hazardous Canyon, we must get to you quick!!

Your racy boy,

L.

Dear M and D,

We are so lucky having Stubbs! He may be just a small scaredycrow, but he keeps being a saver.

We looked and looked for bridges across the Riggly, but no luck. So we thought, Oh well, we'll cross it by log—here's one, paddle, paddle. But no, that river was quick as a zipwire. Zoooooom!! we went, like a twig in a gutter. The rocks were sharp as teeth—lucky we missed them all—and on and on we went rushing, frozz and scared and clinging tight. Then we heard a ROARING. We thought, Oh no, Funder Falls! Will we go

H! E! L! P! splattt?

Answer: Almost, but no. Yeller said,
"QUICK, STUBBY, HELP ME. WE MUST PUT
THE KITE UP IN THE TREES TO TANGLE!"

Stubbs was doing his fastest
beakwork on the cross-sticks, then
WHOOSH! ARRKK! Come back,
Stubbs! But it was 2 late! Up he went,
swoosh, right to the top of a tall oak tree!

Yeller and me held tight on the string
till we came to shore at last. Phew!

We got Stubbs down then—he was a
bit trembly but not hurt. We kept saying,
"Gosh, thanks, Stubbs, that was a daring
deed, Stubbs, you saved our lives, Stubbs,
you really flew there, Stubbs!"

Stubbs just said a shy, "Ark! Ark-
zaggerate!" Meaning that was not real
flying. So modest.

Yours dryingoffly,

L.

Dear M and D,

Yesterday poor old Stubbs woke up sneezy, saying, "Ah-ah-Arkscuse! Ah-ah-Arkscuse!" There was no time for bed and glowworm gargle, because we had to rush to save Smells.

Another big problem at Hazardous Canyon—there is a notice there. It says:

Yeller said, "I KNOW THIS IS A SHORTER WAY THAN GOIN' OVER THE HILLS TO LAKE LEMMIN'. ALL THAT SNOW UP THERE MIGHT FALL ON US."

I said, "Yes, I know, and it might make a big bang."

Then Stubbs went, "Ah–ah–ah–
ARKSCUSE!!!"

So, Bang Rumble Splat! An avalanche
pounced down on us.

Yours sufflocatedly,

L. Wolf

Dear M and D,

Shhh! We are secretly camping in Frettnin Forest. Gosh, escaping from avalanches is hard! I was so proud of Yeller—he hates even touching snow. But Stubbs cawed, "ARK! ARKSCAVATE!" meaning we don't have time for trembling, just hurry up and do tunneling!

It took 4 hours of hard claw and beakwork, with no rest, no snacks, nothing. But then we tunneled blinkingly into the moonshine. And *arrroooo* (pant, pant) for our good old Lake Lemming! And watch out Mister Twister, you cubrobber, because 3 Daring Deeders are coming to get you!

Yours nearly homely,

L.

Dear Mom and Dad,

Back at last, BUT terrible news. The Adventure Academy sign is gone. Now the sign says:

Also, we found chalky X marks on trees everywhere! Why does he want to cut them down? What is that Mister Twister up to?

Your wurrid

L.

Dear M and D,

Adventure Acad has got all new big locks and bars on it. So up we crept peepingly to the kitchen window. And guess what we spied? Smells gagged up and strapped in his high chair! Plus all the gold was on the kitchen table being chinkled gloatingly by A BIG SNEAKY FOX. BOOO!

Not fair! Smells was 2 easy to tempt. He told the combination, just to be a king and a star on TV. And he never got his twinkly crown, even. So crool.

But what can we do to uncapture him? Mister Twister has bags more cunningness than us, plus all the doors and windows are locked tight.

Yours hinderedly,

L.

Dear M and D,

Attacked at midnight!!

Mister Twister saw us doing spying, so he
tried to kill us dead in our tent!

We thought we were tucked up safely in
our secret camp. But no! BOOM!!! BANG!!
My worst terror!! Down came fireballs,
bright and SCREAMING worse than owls.
Even shut eyes could not keep you from
seeing:

blue fireballs, BANG!

red fireballs, BANG!

green fireballs, BANG!

orange fireballs, BANG!

BANG!!!!

I forget most of it now, except rolling in the snow coldly. Then running, running, more like a scaredy hen than a proud wolf cub. Then all was blackness. Then 2 wurrid pointy faces close to mine. Stubbs said, "Ark! Ark-splosion! Ark! Ark-cident!"

Yeller said, "HE FIREWURKED US, LICKLE. YOU BUMPED YOUR HEAD ON A TREE BUT YORE SAFE NOW."

I said, "Oh dear. Sometimes I think Mister Twister is just 2 clever for us. What do you think?"

Yeller said, "GRRRRR. I THINK ENUF IS ENUF."

Yours shockedly,
L. Wolf

Dear Mom and Dad,

Yeller has thought of an ABCD plan. We have done A nearly, which is bending back small trees all around Adventure Academy and tying them down with string, then loading them up with snow lumps (like catapults, get it?!).

It was so hard and dangerous because of Mister Twister on the roof. If he sees us just twitch, he shoots rockets at us! He is a deadly aimer, and he knows bangs are my worst terror. But I did not run away. I must be a brave Arksample to Stubbs, because of Plan B tomorrow.

L.

Dear M and D,

Tonight is up to Stubbs.

Yeller has told him Plan B. Plus he has done a banner to get his braveness up:

ON THIS NIGHT
WITH NO HELP
FROM HOT STEMERS
OR KITES
THE GRATE
STUBBY CROW
WIL FLY

(Toes crossed for no fainting.)

Yeller and me are waiting in our hollow hidytree, ready for a fast race to the back wall of Adventure Acad, then we will tunnel quick into the cellar without Mister Twister seeing.

Stubbs is around in the front now doing his job, keeping Mister Twister's sharp eyes off us. The catapult trees are ready all around, bended back and loaded with snow lumps.

So, Plan B, you are on your marks. Stubbs the Crow, you must fly! Please fly, Stubbs, PLEEEEZ. You can do it!

This could be my last letter, I bet. But you can still say, "Oh well, we are proud of Little and Yeller, because they did not half-try to save our darling baby ~~pest~~ pet."

Farewell from

L. B. Wolf

Dear M and D,

We are IN secretly, and that is 1 big check for PLAN C, tunneling! ✔ Yeller and me tunneled like 2 moles with a ferret chasing them, phew, pant. But a question: Is Stubbs still a scaredycrow, or is he a hero also? Answer: You will soon find out.

Plan B started with me doing flashes with my flashlight, our secret signal for Stubbs to fly quick and snip the catapult strings with his clever beak. But—oh no! Mister Twister saw him doing his taxi run for takeoff. He loudshouted from the roof, "You foolish fledgling, you will never leave the ground! Take that!" Then he shot a big rocket right at him—*WEEE*BOOM—then more and more! Yeller and me thought, Oh no, he has exploded our cheery pal!
But then arrroooooOOOOOOOM!! LIFT OFF!!

Up went Stubbs, faster than the rockets! He caught 2 of them in midair and pointed them back at Mister Twister going *SCREEE*-BLAMM! onto the roof. Arroooo! That gave Mister Twister a sparky taste of his own shocks, har, har!!

Plus Mister Twister was so busy dancing on top of the house that he missed us doing Plan C, digging down.

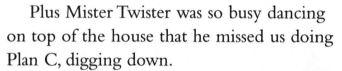

Now we must wait here quiet as slugs before we can do PLAN D.

Yours shhhly,

L.

P.S. Good thing we did tunneling practiss at Hazardous Canyon, huh?

Dear Mom and Dad,

Da-dah, we have rescued Smells! Mister Twister locked himself in the bell tower to keep from being bombed by snow and his own rockets, so we crept into the kitchen and untied the small wiggler.

I 'spect you are really really happy and grateful now, saying, "Arroooo for our Daring Rescue Boy," etc., but Smells did not even say 'Thank you, brave bro.' All he did was bite me, just for taking his gag off. How did I know he likes going *mmm, mmm, mmm?* Also, guess what? Now he says he wants to be a cubnapper like Mister Twister. We have to let him tie us up all the time or he howls his head off. And the worst thing—he has locked all the gold in the safe again and forgotten the combination!!

Mister Twister thinks we are still outside. We can hear him loudshouting to us from the bell tower. Saying things like, "I know you are out there, my boys! Better leave Frettnin Forest immediately. You will never keep me from turning it into a Safari Park. Tomorrow my beavers begin cutting down trees to make room for the highway. And in no time the hunters will be here with their loud guns. So, BANG BANG!"

Ooo-er! Better hurry up and do Plan D! We need some dressing up for it and some cooking smells to tempt that fox down from the bell tower.

So lots to do before midnight.

Your busy boy,

L.

Dear M and D,

All set for Plan D, and it's only 1/2 past 11, so time for a small note to tell about it.

Yeller and me have all our stuff ready:

2 sheets

1 green glowmask

6 pull chains

1 cardboard loudshouter

1 big pair boots
(Uncle Bigbad's old 1's)

1 cooking pot, plus
last 2 cans of bakebeans
(canteen size, yum, yum).

Just before midnight, we will cook the bakebeans. Up will go the lovely smell, and down will come Mister Twister, drool, drool. Then out behind the curtain will come Yeller dressed up as a Boogiebeast. Also I will do a scary voice like this:

I AM THE GHOST OF BIGBAD WOLF.

FLY AND FLEE, FOUL FOX!!

SHOVE OFF TO VILE ISLAND

AND STAY THERE.

AND IF YOU BLINKING BLUNKING DON'T,

I'LL BOIL UP YER WICKED BONES

AND SERVE YER UP AS SOUP!

Then Mister Twister will go, Ooo-er, mercy! And he will run off. Good, hm?

Yours craftily,

L.

Dear M and D,

Plan D went a little bit wrong. This is how.

The cooking part was good. Up went the bakebeany whiff (tempt, tempt). Then down the bell tower steps came Mister Twister (drool, drool). Smells was in his high chair, pretending to be tied up still. I was hiding under the table, and Yeller was hiding behind the curtain dressed up as a Boogiebeast.

In came Mister Twister, and into the pot went the ladle. (Stir, stir, lipsmack, lipsmack.) I thought, Come on, Yeller, hurry up, start shocking!

Then, guess what? Yeller did not come through the curtains. He came through the wall! And he did not have his glowmask on—he had a big furry face instead, plus great big red eyes and great big yellow teeth, plus dribble dribbling down. His eyebrows met in the middle like 2 furry caterpillars. He looked all tall and thin and horrible.

Also, he did not let me say my scary words. He did his own ones, like this:

I AM THE GHOST OF UNCLE BIGBAD!

ME WHO DIED OF THE JUMPING BEANBANGS!

I DROOL, I DROOL FOR A LUVLY GOBFULL!

FETCH ME THE SHOVEL AND FEED ME SWIFTLY!

Mister Twister went white as a polar bear and jumped straight out the window.

So I said, "Wow, Yeller, you were perfect. You have scared Mister Twister away forever, I bet."

Only it was not Yeller. Yeller came out through the curtains in his Boogiebeast outfit. So I said, "Well, who is that with the big red eyes and yellow teeth and dribble dribbling down?"

And Yeller looked

and he saw

and he went

A A A A A A A A A A a a a a a a a a a a a a a a !!

And so did I.

Yours ooo-erly,

L. Wolf

ADVENTURE ACADEMY

Dear M and D,

Arrroooo! Mister Twister is really gone! And 3 arrroooos for Stubbs! Because just as Mister Twister jumped out the window, guess who came flying through? Answer: Stubbs the Crow! What a flyer. He loves it! He says it is Ark! Ark! Ark-zillerating!

Me and Yeller and Smells had all our fur up from scaryness when he flew in. He said, "Ark! Ark-straordinary!" meaning, You all look like you have seen a ghost. Which we had. Imagine Uncle Bigbad coming back from the nice grave I dug for him! I s'pose he came back for a shovelful of bakebeans— he always loved them.

ARROOOOOO°°

Good fun though, hm?

Yours cheerily,

LiHly

Dear Mom and Dad,

It is sooooo nice that Yeller has his old noisy voice back. It was the shock that did it for him.

We have been talking and talking about Adventure Acad. Yeller said, "KNOW WHAT I THINK, LICKLE? I THINK INSTANT ADVENTURE PLAYGROUNDS ARE FOR TAME PETS, NOT FOR BRUTE BEASTS LIKE US."

I said, "Yes, we like getting our braveness up in wild places, don't we?"

Yeller said, "LET'S NOT TEACH DARING DEEDS. LET'S HAVE ANOTHER SORT OF SCHOOL."

I said, "Good idea. But let's have a 1st Prize Day for our best pupil!"

Stubbs said a happy Ark! Ark-zackly! and did a loop-the-loop around the light.

Yours,

L.

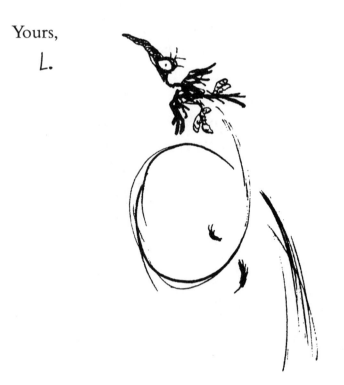

ADVENTURE ACADEMY

FRETTNIN FOREST, BEASTSHIRE
HEADS: LITTLE WOLF AND YELLER WOLF, ESQS

Prize Day

Dear Mom and Dad,

Today us Heads awarded our pupil, Stubbs Crow, the Adventure Academy Cup for High Flyers. His mom and dad were so proud that they brought the whole flock along to caw and flap for him.

Then I gave Yeller his Gold Daring Deed Award for Braveness in a Blizzard. And guess what? The Gold Daring Deed Award for Braveness against Bangs went to L. Wolf, Esqwire. Also, the Silver DD Award for Clues and Courage while Cubnapped went to Smellybreff Wolf.

123

It's a shame that awards do not keep small bros from being painy. He likes pretending to be Uncle Bigbad all the time, so he makes me feed him bakebeans with a shovel or no peace. So today I gave him a good bossing. I said, "Behave, Smells! The bakebeans are all gone! Now we must buy more! But you have locked up all the gold. If you want bakebeans, just hurry up and remember that combination!"

No good me being Headly. All that did was make him be nasty to get me back. He is hiding somewhere, and he has taken the safe with him. When I catch him, I will probly go RAVING MAD at him like Dad.

Yours grrrly,

L.

Dear M and D,

I found Smells. He was in the garden with the safe, plus Mister Twister's leftover rockets. He stuffed all the rockets under the safe and lit them.

Good thing I am a hero about bangs now. Because Smells's 1 went

KERBLAMMM CHINKLE CHINKLE!!

Smells says he only wanted to open the safe for bakebean money. He did not mean to blow it all over Frettnin Forest, but it's a little bit late now. It took us all day finding just 2 gold pieces.

Also, Smells has blown his sailor suit off, plus his tailfur. But do not fear and fret. Stubbs has glued some gray bear fluff on him for now.

Yours with ears dinging,

L.

Dear M and D,

Good old Smells. He gave us a
BRILLIANT new idea.

We will start up a new scary school for
brute beasts. Our teaching will be Hunting
and Haunting. We will do Hunting for Gold
in the daytime, plus Horror Haunting in the
nighttime. We will play Hello Ween and have
midnight feasts of bakebeans (canteen size).
That will tempt back the ghost of Uncle
Bigbad, so then he can teach us Walking
through Walls, Shocking for Beginners, etc.
Stubbs can teach Spooksuit Making and
Flying Lessons. And Smells can be a small
horror, and our new school will be called
Haunted Hall, the Spookiest School in the
World!!!

Yr xcited

Little

HAUNTED HALL
FOR SMALL HORRORS

Dear Mom and Dad,

Me, Yeller, Stubbs, and Smells are waiting for midnight. We have all got our spooksuits and glowmasks on. Also, the bakebeans are going *bubble bubble* in the pot. Hmmm, nice! Uncle Bigbad's ghost will appear soonly, and then the fun can start!!!

Yours spookingly,

Little

HAUNTED HALL
FOR SMALL HORRORS

Dear Mom and Dad,

I have filled up Yeller's book now, so I am going to do LITTLE WOLF'S DIARY OF DARING DEEDS in all different colors on the front of it. That means I am the bet winner—Yeller owes me 3 trillions of yummy grub! So hurry up, Springtime, and hurry up, parents, to come for a nice scary midnight feast. From now on, the shocks are on me!

AWHHHHHOOOOOOOOOOOOOOOOOOOOOOOOO!
from